FIRST CHASM
A Simple Harpy Hunt

The Blood Chasms of Illustrander
#1

FIRST CHASM
A Simple Harpy Hunt

The Blood Chasms of Illustrander
#1

By Michael G. Karabinis

Table of Contents

FIRST CHASM: A SIMPLE HARPY HUNT
The Blood Chasms of Illustrander #1

Acknowledgments

Several people helped me in the creation of this little story—as is the case with most written projects. Mostly in the form of bouncing ideas off of them or using them—unbeknownst to them—as inspiration for my characters and their personalities.

A special thank you to my good friend, Khaled Assaf, whose input has been more invaluable to me than he realizes, and to my family, whose heartfelt enthusiasm for my work has been extremely encouraging.

Even though many people have helped me on this trip, only one has done so directly, with writing it. That person has been with me since the conception of my novel's story to the editing and publishing of this very novella. I improved at writing in no small part due to her feedback and influence. That person is my best friend and fellow aspiring author, Loksanor, who also happens to be my critique partner, editor, and cover illustrator.
Thank you, for putting up with my constant bickering about writing this whole time. I wouldn't have done it without you.

First Chasm:
A Simple Harpy Hunt
The Blood Chasms of Illustrander #1

Daren stepped out of the small cavern the Sin Binders of his squad had used as a shelter for the cold, rainy night. "Good morning," he said to Armon, who had the last watch and was already waiting outside, backpack thrown over his right shoulder.

Armon's answer was a lazy bob of the head, barely acknowledging Daren's presence.

"Right," Daren shrugged off Armon's disregard. "Always a pleasure," he commented absently as he walked past him toward his horse. "I'm afraid that you'll have to wait for me here," Daren said to the mare, petting its gray mane. "Karnerk Rise is no place for a delicate lady like you." He winked, the mare retorting with an annoyed snort.

Daren chuckled, but before he could continue the silly exchange, his eyes were drawn by the horizon beyond the edge of the rocky path. The dark blues of the night had started being replaced by the various oranges and yellows of the morn as the sun had begun its daily routine, scarring the hazy atmosphere with its rays.

Daren whistled, beholden. "Now, *that's* a sight," he revered, letting his backpack drop on a patch of dry rocks that he'd noted earlier, as he found himself involuntarily walking toward the steep edge.

The only reminders of last night's storm were a few clouds that still persisted overhead, the slickness of the rocks under his boots, and the scent of wet soil that hung in the air, which Daren always regarded as pleasant and refreshing. During their ride here, he could hardly see anything beyond his nose, but now that the weather had cleared up…

Hands trembling, Daren clenched his fists. *Is this what my life will entail from now on?* he wondered, silently, unable to hold back a broad smile from spreading across his face. *Is this what life looks like, outside Illustrander?* His eyes teared for a moment but, by taking a deep, shuddering breath, he managed to suppress the impulse.

Karnerk Rise was the highest mountain range on the continent. That, Daren, knew, but no one had ever prepared him for such an incredible view. The entire Basin of Aellus seemed to be laid before him; the sun was getting brighter and brighter with each passing moment, rising beyond the mountain peaks of Ekthra on the opposite side. From this distance, through the after-storm morning haze, and despite the sun's aid in outlining the mount, it looked more of a distant smudge over the horizon than a distinguishable landmark. Equally opaque were the snow-covered Ridge of Bjergegory, which covered the northern part of the

Basin, and the mist-covered lands of the Wounded Vale that dominated the south.

The natural canvas was dotted by the majestic city of Illustrander at the center. With its five, pure white Towers of marble that were linked together by grand walls of dark granite, forming a somewhat asymmetric square that extended across hundreds of miles, covering a good section of the plains. Farmlands, evident by the smoother, more cultivated colors of green and yellow around them, spread tightly alongside the outer rim of the capital's gigantic walls. The most impressive part of it all was the grandeur of the Pale Towers, whose peaks, always obscured by thick clouds, seemed to rise indefinitely, dwarfing everything around.

The world was vast and endless, and although in the grand scheme of things the Basin of Aellus was but a speck of dust under the wide sky's hand, the city of Illustrander could be seen as a silver ring, adorning it.

"Impressive, ain't it?" said Master Sergeant Fran, breaking Daren out of his reverie.

Daren was so entranced by the view that he had failed to notice the approaching heavy footsteps of the stocky, old man. "Yes, Master Sergeant, Sir," he rushed a reply.

"Bah! Cut that crap," the Master Sergeant said, brashly. "You don't need to address me by my full honorific. Sergeant will do. You can revert to full titles once we are back home, though by then, you'll be an officer; way above *my* payroll. You academy-grown kids always are." He said that with a surprisingly wide smile. "Besides, if we were strictly talking rank here, I should be the one addressing you as 'Sir.'"

"Yes, Sergeant," Daren agreed, smiling. Once Daren was done with this contract, his first contract, he would be officially accepted into the ranks of the Sin Binders and, as the Master Sergeant had pointed out, he would be awarded his first real rank, that of a Second Lieutenant, the first rank of an officer. *Not much longer now,* he remarked to himself.

"Don't encourage him, old man. He is not ready—he'll never be," Armon snarled as he passed the two men, sweeping black strands of hair away from his frowning forehead.

"Pay him no mind, pretty boy," Anthia joined in, coming up behind Armon. Her voice resembled a cooing dove, in contrast to Armon's clunking hen. "He is just bitter, cause I rejected him." She winked, hazel irises reflecting the oranges of the sunrise.

Armon scoffed, and although he didn't refute her statement, Daren could tell that Anthia was joking. He knew the two to be childhood friends.

Master Sergeant Fran barked a laugh, slamming a heavy hand on Daren's shoulder.

Surprised by the strength of the gesture, Daren lost his balance and would have probably fallen over the edge if Anthia hadn't grabbed him by the red stripe that hung on his back.

"Good luck with that one, boy, you'll need it," Master Sergeant Fran joked, though Daren wasn't sure whether he was referring to Armon's disdain or Anthia's flirty advances.

Armon grunted, crossing his arms. "He'll never make it," he grumbled.

The Master Sergeant's dark eyes stayed on Armon for a long moment, stroking at his bushy mustache. He seemed oblivious to the accident he had almost caused. "That boy…" he murmured, shaking his head, then with a shrug, he took the lead in front of Armon. "Time to get moving, Binders!" He waved forward. "We got a long way ahead of us, still."

Anthia giggled, and with another wink, gestured forward.

Daren watched her go. As expected of a Sin Binder, Anthia's physique was superb, her pace was solid and assured, yet alluring and elegant—despite the heavy backpack on her shoulder. Her white and red uniform was identical to that of Daren's except for the fact that it came with a small overskirt around the waist and she wore her boots outside tight pants, while Daren's, male counterpart, had loose pants covering the boots. The three long braids that adorned the left side of her short, dark hair—traditional woman's styling in Illustrander that indicated social status, age, and marriage availability—told Daren that she wasn't married and that she would be somewhere between twenty to twenty-four years old, just a little older than he was.

Daren rushed to pick up his backpack, and after sparing a short moment to bid farewell to his horse, he quickly dashed forward to catch up to his squad, falling in place behind Anthia.

As she smiled back at him over her shoulder, Daren found himself blushing. *By the Pale Towers, she is stunning.* He ran an anxious, gloved hand over his dark-brown hair, but looking down at it, he frowned. *More hairs, huh? And I'm not even twenty yet...* Daren had been seeing his hair thinning more and more lately. He let out a resigned sigh. *Whatever, if it goes, it goes.* He shrugged, wiggling his fingers to allow the breeze to take the hairs away. *Guess, I'll have to shave it off completely, and... maybe grow a beard to compensate.* At that thought, Daren smiled to himself. He liked the idea of growing a beard, it was something that he'd always wanted to do. So far he had been forced to follow the standard military protocol of shaving his face every morning, but once he was a full-fledged Sin Binder, he wouldn't have to abide by such rules, at least not so strictly.

"You are falling behind, boy!" Master Sergeant Fran called.

Daren startled. "Coming, Sir!"

The path to the top was treacherous, if an amalgam of rocks, boulders, and the occasional thorned bush could be called a path that is, far more treacherous than Daren had anticipated. He hadn't expected it to be easy, but neither did he imagine it would be so exasperating. The view of the Basin was still magnificent, of course, but the cold air that pierced his exposed face like thousands of needles, as well as the increasing tirade of his breathing, kind of stole the magic of the moment away. The weather conditions inside Illustrander were favorable throughout the entire year, and Daren had never felt this kind of intrusive cold before in his life.

Hands braced on his knees for support, Daren sucked in a breath of fresh air, the coldness of which felt like ice cubes crumbling down his throat. They had been climbing for no more than a couple of hours, yet Daren felt like he had been at it for days. "Something's not right," he muttered, wearily.

"Sir!" Anthia called, having noticed Daren's pause.

Master Sergeant Fran looked back. "Need a break, boy?" the old Binder asked, the movement of his lips indicated only by the bouncy waving of his bushy mustache.

Armon grunted, darting his eyes toward Daren.

Daren waved a hand. "No, Sir. I can keep going," he beckoned, standing tall and puffing his chest with a well-hidden effort. Thankfully, his false-boasting was unsuccessful.

Master Sergeant Fran nodded. "Alright, let us take a quarter to rest," he ordered, to Armon's disapproval.

"Such a waste of time," Armon scoffed, pointedly.

"Oh, come now. It's normal for him to run out of breath at this height," Anthia condoned.

"Like I have been saying," Armon growled back. *"Not, ready!"*

"Wait," Daren interjected, "what do you mean, it's normal?"

"At this elevation, the air we breathe is much thinner, boy. Your training grades, which I hear are on the high end of the scale, have nothing to do with this fact. The lack of oxygen can easily overpower even the mightiest of us," Master Sergeant Fran explained at length.

That's when Daren noticed, for the first time, that none of his three companions seemed tired. They showed no signs of weariness or even of sweat on them. "I'm guessing that this is not your first time on Karnerk Rise?" he asked, sweeping his eyes across the three.

"Far from it," Anthia said, a hint of pride in her tone. "Almost all of our contracts are for this side of the Basin, with the occasional oddball here and there. We serve the Western Pale Tower, you see, so Karnerk Rise is under our jurisdiction."

"I see…" Daren nodded, turning his gaze toward the Western Pale Tower, which was the closest to them. He didn't need to wonder which Tower *he* would be stationed at when this was over. All academy-grown Sin Binders were used in rotation between all the Towers, with the South Pale Tower, the one closest to the mist-covered lands of the Wounded Vale, as their final destination. That area housed the largest Blood Chasm on the continent. The Academy, where Daren had lived his entire life until now, was housed inside the central Pale Tower, at the heart of Illustrander, also known as the 'Pillar' of Illustrander. Though it didn't seem all that peculiar from this distance, there were two key differences when compared to the other four towers. It was square, as opposed to circular, and as wide as all four of them combined. It almost looked like a smaller Illustrander inside Illustrander, its four sides mirroring the great granite walls. The mightiest of the Penta-Pantheon resided at its top; Archon Feomathdar.

"Just look at him," Armon scowled, setting his back on a boulder and crossing his arms. "He doesn't even know with whom he is traveling... It may be a simple harpy hunt but you could have done *some* research, you know," he sneered at Daren.

Daren's patience with Armon's constant, unprovoked disdain, had reached its limit. "What exactly is your problem, *Corporal?*" he mocked, emphasizing Armon's rank as it was the second lowest of the non-commissioned officer ranks: three ranks below the Master Sergeant and *five* ranks below Daren's destined one, of second lieutenant. Even Daren's current, transitory rank of 'Warrant Officer' was higher on the hierarchy than a corporal's. In fact, it was one rank higher than even that of Master Sergeant's. The only reason Daren was even following Master Sergeant Fran's orders was due to Fran being the appointed Squad Leader.

Daren had been holding back on that insult for a while now, and judging by the red color that Armon's face swiftly adopted, it had landed on just the right spot.

To Daren's satisfaction, Armon directed his eyes away, without replying, his jaw tightly clenched. Just as Daren had suspected, Armon's real issues with him were not on a personal level but were rather rooted in the infrastructure of military ascendancy. As an academy-grown Sin Binder, Daren would begin his career as an officer, while it would take Armon a lifetime to reach that prestige. It was common for Sin Binders of Armon's upbringing to consider it insulting to be outranked by someone so much younger and inexperienced than themselves.

"Rawr," Anthia purred. "I've never seen anyone silence Armon so promptly." Her gaze felt like a heated blade hovering over Daren's skin, taunting. Fortunately for Daren, his blush was covered this time around by his already red cheeks, which was the natural result of the high elevation.

"You know," Daren sighed, feeling a sting of guilt for mocking Armon about something he had no power over. "I get it. I really do…"

Armon turned toward Daren again, interested.

"I may not have the same experience on the field as you do," Daren continued, "but I have been in training for as long as I can remember, and unlike you, I never had a choice in the matter. Not that I have any regrets, but the academy is the only family I've ever known—if you could even call *that* a family." He grinned. "To be honest, I have no idea as to what a family really is. I only know the theory of it. To top it off, Illustrander is the only place I've ever been to. Until now that is, and—"

"And," Anthia interrupted, saving Daren from further self-deprecation. She leaned forward, hands clasped behind her back, and looked sideways at Daren with a warm smile. She winked, turning to address Armon. "Whether you like it or not, my dear Armon, we are not here for a… how did you put it? 'A simple harpy hunt,' but rather to guide and support a Warrant Officer through his transition to officership, under the guise of one. Don't downplay our job, show some respect… and understanding. Let's not forget that we are talking about a potential 'Pledge Bearer' here, shall we?"

Armon didn't reply, though his frown seemed to have softened a bit.

"Speaking of which," Master Sergeant Fran intercepted. If the upside-down crescent shape of his mustache was of any indication, he had been smiling this whole time. "Let's talk about that, eh?" He bumped his thick eyebrows as he settled down.

Daren welcomed the change of subject. The sudden mention of Pledge Bearers wasn't something that he liked to think about, not yet anyway. He was still too early in his career, though he *did* know that it would be a role that he would be called upon to fulfill eventually, like all academy-grown officers. Instead, he focused his attention on their current contract; their ultimate goal was to clear a nest of harpies that had been causing problems for the cattle herders in the area, but no further details had been given before that.

"So, tell me, boy. What do you know about harpies?"

"Well, Sir," Daren paused, realizing, "not much, to be honest. Bird-like, human heads, live in flocks." He shrugged. "We only studied their bestiary entries briefly, and it has been years since then."

"Not surprising," Armon said, though this time there was no undertone of sarcasm or disdain in his voice. "Harpies are nothing more than over-bloated chickens with ugly mugs."

"And breasts, don't forget them, little bobbles," Anthia added, jokingly, drawing everyone attention.

Armon winced, and after a short moment of silence. "'Bobbles?' Anthia, really?"

Anthia gave a nonchalant shrug.

"There's one thing that doesn't make sense," Daren mused aloud, tapping his lips with one finger while ignoring the comments of his companions.

The Master Sergeant grinned at Daren, squinting his dark eyes, expectantly.

"If I am not mistaken, harpies are scavengers, living off of carcasses of dead animals…" Daren trailed off. "May I take a look at our contract?" he asked, presenting an open palm.

Master Sergeant Fran slid a gloved hand under the wide, single-sided, red leather pauldron on his left and pulled out a small metallic cylinder. He casually threw it over to Anthia, who stood closest to Daren, and she in turn passed it on to him.

Daren unscrewed the cylinder, dividing it into two pieces, and unwrapped the papyrus lying within. "Scavenging creatures like harpies would attack a human settlement only in dire desperation, and even in those, rare cases, they would only do away with a couple of animals at a time," he said, scanning the contents of the contract. "Yet, the report here says they have been attacking numerous herds in the surrounding areas, with more than a dozen animals killed or carried away in the span of a week." He looked up at the old Binder. "Either we are dealing with an unusually large flock, which doesn't seem very plausible, considering how uneventful our trip has been so far, or the creatures have suddenly decided to go against their nature and act boldly."

Master Sergeant's grin widened, to the point that Daren even managed a glimpse of his white teeth underneath the mustache. "Good catch, boy. That is an excellent observation. I'm glad that you are not seeing this task as a minor inconvenience, like some other…" He shot a judgemental glance over both Armon and Anthia. "…more experienced Binders do."

Armon looked away, muttering something under his breath.

Anthia on the other hand, giggled, trapping her tongue between teeth as she scratched the back of her head.

"You should take this more seriously," Master Sergeant Fran scolded. "Just because there are no Blood Chasms on Karnerk Rise, it doesn't mean that there are no dangers." He turned to Daren, his expression softening. "You are right about the implausibility of a large flock," the old Binder continued. "We already know where they are nesting and their numbers certainly don't match those suggested by our reports, which are no older than a ten-day. So, either they managed to multiply tenfold in the span of a few days, or there's something else at play here."

"What could it be, Sir?" Daren asked, feeling a creeping mood of excitement engulf him, now that his observations had been so soundly confirmed.

"That, boy, we have to find out on our own," the old Binder said, rising to his feet. "Get ready, Binders. Check your equipment, we may need to leave our backpacks behind at a moment's notice. We wouldn't want them, ugly chickens, to catch us in our underpants, would we?"

Daren didn't need to follow that order since he had already been in full gear, with only provisions in his backpack. Instead, he directed his attention to the kind of weaponry his companions had been carrying.

Unlike the Paladins of Illustrander that patrolled and guarded the inner walls of the city, or the various town Militia of the surrounding provinces, Sin Binder's set of equipment was personalized for each individual. Though, they *did* follow a set of guidelines, like their uniform of white and red or the mandatory use of silver or gold-coated weapons and chains—tied on the right armband—as pure metals were effective against certain types of vampire and various incorporeal Chasmals, like wraiths and banshees. Daren always found the variety of arsenal to be fascinating, and a good indicator as to where each Binder had been trained.

Regardless of where he currently served, Master Sergeant Fran had clearly been taught in the North, where brawn and raw strength were favored. His greataxe was of no particular interest to Daren, as he'd never cared much for such unwieldy things. Nevertheless, it certainly matched the imposing physique of its wielder.

Armon and Anthia, with their sleek figures and light swords, came from the Western Pale Tower, where finesse and quickness were endorsed. Armon especially, was the definition of that discipline. He was an ambidextrous duelist, indicated by two, curved, single-edged shortswords adorning his belt. Yet, despite the rarity of Armon's talent of wielding two weapons at the same time, Anthia was the one that drew Daren's attention the longest.

Being a Fencer, Anthia was wearing a stunning, slender sword that outmatched her beauty. It had an incredibly intricate, golden guard with a spiral shape extending forward from the crosspiece, offering protection to the hand from all directions; a rapier. Looking at it, Daren tapped the guard of his much humbler, longsword in its red sheath, as if soothing its pain. *Don't worry, you'll always be special to me,* he comforted. Daren had owned that sword since he was fifteen, the reward for winning a combat tournament at the academy. *Though, we could always put a prettier crossguard on you, eh?* He smiled, looking down at it, as the image of the upgrade began to take shape in his mind. Normally, a crossguard similar to that of a rapier wouldn't be ideal for a two-handed grip which his longsword was mainly designed for, and the added weight on the handle would affect the balance of the blade, but Daren knew he could make it work—with a few tweaks. Besides, his low on the ground fighting style could even benefit from such a design, as his hands were often too exposed for his liking, especially when shifting between knees during combos.

Tapping again at his sword, Daren averted his gaze toward the breathtaking view of the Basin of Aellus. The sun had climbed higher over the horizon and had dispersed the morning haze. Its warmth would have been a welcomed addition to the assault of sensations on Daren's face and lungs, seeing how those sensations varied from cold to… *really cold.* Luckily, it wasn't a windy day. Daren could have only imagined the horrors a breeze would be carrying. A hand fell on his shoulder, the sturdiness of which could only have belonged to the Master Sergeant.

"Take one last peek of the Basin, boy. For we will soon be leaving it behind." The old Binder gestured upward, along the ridge. "We are going to turn around that outcropping, to the blind side of the mount." He tapped Daren's shoulder two more times and turned to take the lead.

Watching the Master Sergeant go, Daren sniffed and then proceeded to rub his nose maniacally, trying to combat the numbness. He paused, noticing from the corner of his eye, Anthia's purposeful approach. The position he was frozen in, nose pinched upward with his palm, drew a few cute giggles from her.

"You can use the back stripe, you know."

Daren turned to her, "back stripe?"

"Yeah, the—" she paused, smiling. "Here, let me..." She reached for the stripe of cloth hanging over Daren's single-sided pauldron. Closer in terms of look to that of an officer, it was red, with a golden thread outlining the edges, as opposed to the plain white of non-officer ranks. It was an emblematic indication of rank, simple and easy to notice from a distance; white for none-officers, red for officers up to the captain rank, and after that, multiple stripes of both red and white, reaching up to a total of six for a high general.

Anthia took the red stripe with delicate, gloved fingers, and standing on toes, started wrapping it around Daren's neck, slowly, in unnecessarily wide motions, as if savoring the moment, all the while wearing a warm smile across her lips.

Daren swallowed, bewildered by Anthia's natural beauty. She was so close to him that he could feel her warmth washing over him with each arc her hands made over his head. Even her scent, which wasn't exactly the flowery type, managed to make its way into his numb nostrils. The smell of tanned leather and steel, that of a Sin Binder's uniform. *Say something, you fool,* Daren prodded himself. He wasn't unfamiliar with a woman's touch, but the few encounters he'd had so far were in the form of paid services, a practice which he had never come to terms with. *"A necessary evil,"* his colleagues had kept reminding him.

"There," Anthia said, having finished the knot, "better now?" She let her hands slide down slowly as she shifted her weight from booted toes to heels.

Daren blinked a few times, immediately feeling the warmth on his mouth and nose. "Yeah, thanks." It really *was* better, seeing as the cloth of which the uniform was made of was known to be fairly resistant to environmental influences, both cold and hot. Why hadn't he thought of this earlier? Part of him, a *big* part of him, was glad that he hadn't.

"Great." Anthia smiled, then turned to walk away.

"Um, Anthia?" Daren managed to stutter.

"Yeah?"

"Uhh, thanks," Daren said, scratching the back of his ear, unable to hold her gaze. "For earlier I mean. For the backing you offered when Armon was being…"

"Himself?" Anthia finished his sentence.

Daren chuckled. "Yeah."

"Think nothing of it," she smiled. "Unlike Armon, I understand how it all must be for you. Having lived your entire life inside Illustrander, you were trapped between four walls. Regardless of how majestic or reassuring, they may have seemed, nothing compares to what's out here, nothing compares to the freshness of the breeze, the scent of the grass, or the…" she trailed off, shaking her head, then continued, soberly. "Everyone claims that Illustrander is the jewel of the country or even the world." She scoffed, piercing Daren with glittering, hazel eyes. "They have no idea what they are talking about."

Daren blinked a few times. "You… seem to have very strong feelings about that."

Anthia sighed, waving a hand. "It's… nothing. I may be overreacting a bit." She smiled. "Becoming a Sin Binder changed my life, gave me purpose, direction, and more importantly, freedom." A meaningful pause. "Freedom is priceless, Daren."

Daren raised a brow. "Now, I'm curious," he said, as a sudden interest that went beyond her outlook flared within him.

"Maybe we can trade tales when this is over then," Anthia said, smiling. "I know of a great place that overlooks the Market district."

Daren smiled back. "I'd like that."

"Hey, kids! You coming or what?" Master Sergeant Fran called.

Both Anthia and Daren perked at the sound of the old Binder's stern voice, breaking themselves free of the moment. "Right away, Sir!"

***

An hour later, they had reached the 'blind side'—as Master Sergeant Fran had called it—of Karnerk Rise. It wasn't difficult to tell where this part of the mountain had gotten its name from. Daren hadn't noticed it before as he didn't have something to compare it to, but the rock formations so far had been relatively smooth to the touch, the deteriorating result of countless rains and winds over the years on the side of the Basin exposed to the open skies. This side of the mountain though, the blind side, seemed to have gotten far less of that treatment. The rock formations here were ragged, angry things, larger in scope, and darker in shade. The vegetation was more vibrant and thick; thorny bushes had been allowed to tap on more of their potential with some of them reaching even higher than Daren would... on a horse's saddle. The large expanse of pine and cypress trees that spread all around them gave the scenery a much different look than the previously lifeless, and steep slopes. Daren quickly decided that, in its own way, this sight was equal in beauty to that of the Basin.

Passing by, Anthia winked. "Freedom, remember?"

How right she was, Daren realized. When the sun's rays had illuminated the Basin of Aellus this morning, Daren had thought it was the most impressive landscape he could ever hope to witness in his life, only to have that viewpoint completely falsified mere hours later. *Just, how much is out there?* he wondered, feeling his heart thumping, excitedly. The jagged, irregular formations of rock, boulder, and tree seemed to be stretching across all directions, further than the eye could see. It was beautiful, majestic even, in a wild, natural way. The air was damper here, making the cold more bearable and less intrusive, though Daren was unwilling to undo the knot Anthia had so tenderly wrapped around his neck, as he had grown to like the feeling of the cloth—it really *was* high-quality material.

The far-distanced mountain peaks that were visible were covered with a white layer of... well, *something*. He tilted his head, curiously. *It couldn't be... snow, could it?*

Anthia giggled. "I was waiting for this."

"What?" Daren started. "Waiting for what?"

"That." She bobbed her head. "That look on your face."

"I don't follow..."

Armon passed by Daren with a knowing smile on his face.

Anthia giggled again. "You were staring at the snowy peaks."

"Snowy peaks…" he echoed in a low voice. He opened his eyes wide. "That's actually snow? I thought that only Bjergegory Ridge had snow."

Master Sergeant Fran barked a laugh. "Of course you did," he said, padding Daren on the shoulder, but didn't elaborate further.

Anthia smiled at Daren, only this time, her smile irritated him. It was the kind of smile you'd give to a young boy, before teaching him how to put on his shoes. She noticed Daren's frown and cleared her throat. "It's a little inside joke for us," she explained, softly. "You are not the first Pillar trainee to join us for a mission, and every time we reach the blind side of Karnerk Rise, we are met with the same reaction."

Daren realized that Anthia hadn't intended to belittle him. He grinned. "So… I guess that snow does not necessarily emanate from frost giants and winter wraiths."

Anthia chuckled. "Probably not." She squeezed Daren's arm lightly. "Don't feel bad about it, not your fault. The only visible patch of snow from Illustrander is Bjergegory Ridge. It makes sense for the people living inside the capital to come up with a bunch of theories about frost giants and wraiths. Though, I firmly believe that the students of Pillar Academy shouldn't be allowed to be swayed by such nonsense. It's ridiculous, especially considering that we are talking about future officers. Still, the blame doesn't lie with you, but the instructors of the Academy." She looked up at him. "Once, I was the same, you know?" She winked.

Daren nodded and turned to look at the far peaks again. He smiled contentedly to himself. *'Freedom' huh?*

∗∗∗

The change of scenery and milder conditions seemed to have affected the party's banter too, though it could also be the increasing familiarity between them. Anthia was actively looking for idle chatter with Daren and had kept finding numerous opportunities for physical contact, from a casual hand on the shoulder, to a playful shove. Unfortunately, Daren didn't make for a good playmate as he had kept finding himself at a loss for words near her. Master Sergeant Fran had always been pleasant enough to interact with but had now dropped the overly professional, stern tone in his voice. Even Armon seemed to have softened a bit, especially when Daren had shown some interest in his twin blades.

A short time later, Daren's attention was drawn to a large hill on his right. He should have noticed it earlier, but hadn't, partly due to constantly watching his step and partly due to the naturally limited view the terrain offered. A large formation spanned across that hill, an area of brighter colored rocks and thicker greenery. Daren cocked his head. *A village?*

"Indeed," Master Sergeant Fran answered Daren's unspoken question. "That is where we are heading: Gierna."

"I didn't know there were habitable settlements this high up the mountain," Daren said.

"There aren't," the Master Sergeant corrected. "Not unless you consider this unruly combination of ruin and refuse to be habitable."

"Curious," Daren said, inducing a raised eyebrow on the old Binder's face. "It's a large village, or at least it was. Yet, there are no roads or pathways leading to it." An easy observation to make due to the arrangement of the ruins being laid before Daren. "Not even a hint of ever existing."

Master Sergeant Fran smiled, approvingly. "Another excellent observation," he praised. "It would have been easy to dismiss the lack of visible pathways since Gierna has been abandoned for hundreds of years, but you are right, we never found any evidence of commuting infrastructure. All our research of the ruins suggests that Gierna was a self-governed, self-maintained community, completely cut-off from the rest of the world."

"Well, it's not too difficult to imagine how that would have worked," Daren noted. "The verdure on that hill suggests good soil and humidity. They could have easily grown crops and raised cattle." He nodded. "Easily defensible too."

"Indeed," Master Sergeant Fran confirmed. "They seemed to have even worshiped their own deities, a full Pantheon of their own. Sadly, very little is left of that part of Gierna's history or her people."

"Probably some sort of Fae creature or maybe even Fae magic itself," Daren speculated, absently.

Master Sergeant Fran barked a hearty laugh. "I like you, boy."

"You got a good eye for that sort of thing, Daren," Anthia complimented.

"Hehe, you think?" Daren said, scratching the back of his head. "I mean, it seemed pretty obvious—"

"Shh!" Armon interrupted. "Do you hear that?" he whispered, raising a finger.

There was a sound lingering in the air, a whimpering. *A cry?* Daren started toward it. *A child's cry!* He tensed, his instincts compelling him to rush toward it, but a hand on the shoulder gave him pause. This hand wasn't heavy and commanding like that of Master Sergeant's, nor was it delicate like Anthia's… *Armon?*

Armon gestured beyond some bushes and under the outcropping they had been standing on, then proceeded to slowly crouch his way there, signaling for Daren to do the same. Anthia and the Master Sergeant, in the same crouched stance, had already started moving from the sides at a wider angle.

How can they be so calm when there is a child in distress? Daren thought but, with a frustrated shake of his head, decided to follow his more experienced companion's lead. He moved beside Armon who had crawled under a thornbush and raised his head to get a glimpse of the source of the sound. Daren could just make out the outline of a woman's head, poking out between two large boulders, swaying back and forth in highly agitated movements, the light-auburn strands of her hair wavering as if influenced by a constant breeze. *Is she holding a child in her lap?* From this angle, Daren could only see the woman's head. The cry of the child suddenly turned into a weeping, and that in turn quickly changed into a scream—a blood-curdling scream. Daren stiffened. The pain that scream conveyed sent chills down his spine. It was indescribable, and Daren thought he could almost feel it, just beneath his skin.

Armon set a hand on Daren's shoulder again, silently reminding him to get a hold of himself. He gestured toward the woman, in a way that suggested to Daren he should get a closer look.

Daren nodded. By crawling a bit further up the ground, he managed to get a more complete view of the woman's naked, upper body. He could make out her exposed neckline and shoulder blades, as well as her spine, which bent beautifully with each spasming movement she made. Her shoulders and hands seemed covered by a stunning collection of colorful feathers. The transition from skin to feather was so seamless that it almost looked like they had grown out of her flesh—they *did* grow out of her flesh, and those were not hands, they were wings! *A harpy?* No, harpies were supposed to be ugly and disgusting, and there were no records of them imitating human voices. This creature, whatever it was, was beautiful and mesmerizing—if a bit unsettling.

"It's a Gamayun," Armon said and although he did so in a whisper, there was a clear undertone of amazement in his voice. "Incredibly rare."

Anthia jumped down near the creature, seemingly unafraid, the Gamayun turned sharply to her.

Daren moved to stand up but Armon held him back again. "Calm down," he sneered. "Gamayun are harmless, if you know how to treat them." He nodded toward Anthia. "Watch and learn."

Anthia took a step toward the creature and offered a deep, elegant curtsey, by crossing her legs and closing her eyes, the tips of her fingers holding the over-the-pants-skirt of her uniform to the sides. A moment later, Master Sergeant Fran also jumped down and bowed to the Gamayun, with one hand on his stomach and the other on his back. He then signaled for Daren and Armon to approach and do the same.

The Gamayun didn't seem bothered at all by the party's presence. It continued its strangely frantic movements and whispered imitations, often bursting into momentary screams. It had the torso and head of a beautiful woman, or at least it resembled such. At closer inspection, Daren could tell that its skin didn't act naturally; there was no flexibility to it. When the mouth moved he couldn't make out any muscles assisting it and its breasts,

36

her breasts? were stiff and nipple-less. From the waist and down it resembled a colorfully-feathered bird of prey, with intimidating talons and a long tail, very similar to that of a peafowl.

Despite its bizarre anatomy, Daren found the Gamayun to be stunningly beautiful. "What an incredible creature," he awed in a low voice.

"Take a good look at it, boy," Master Sergeant Fran said. "I highly doubt you will ever get another chance like this."

"Avian hybrids are common on Karnerk Rise," Anthia explained. "But Gamayun are some of the rarest Fae creatures in existence. No matter how unsettling it might seem, this is a once in a lifetime opportunity. A great honor to meet one." She smiled, eyes sparkling in awe.

Amazing, Daren thought, moving closer. It was short, reaching just above Daren's elbows. The Gamayun barely registered his presence; it kept whispering and throwing its head around, gaze wandering. Its light-auburn curls seemed to be moving on their own volition, wavering in all directions.

This was Daren's third day outside Illustrander's influence and he had already witnessed a plethora of wonders. *From stunning scenery and charming comrades,* Daren thought, smiling, as he looked to Anthia who was still flabbergasted by the Gamayun, *to mythical creatures.* Still smiling, he removed his right glove and reached toward the creature, wondering what the ruins of Gierna could be holding for them next.

"No, wait!" Anthia cried.

At the touch of Daren's fingers on its feathers, the Gamayun snapped its neck toward him, its avian eyes wide, turning from yellow to liquid blue. It let out a powerful scream that knocked Daren over, the creature jumping on top of him immediately after.

Anthia reached for her rapier, but the Master Sergeant raised a hand to halt her. "But..." she started to complain.

"It's too late," Master Sergeant Fran said, firmly. "Let it play out."

Daren found himself unable to move, the Gamayun feeling unnaturally heavy on his chest. It brought its beautiful face up close to Daren's, its small nose touching his, and just as he had suspected, its skin was hard and cold to the touch, like porcelain. They stayed like that for a brief moment. The blue pupils of its eyes looked as if they were rippling, like water on a lake's surface, the irises being the epicenter of the activity. Its breath smelled surprisingly pleasant, like grass or old leaves, an odor that Daren knew was often associated with creatures that had ties to the Realm of Fae, but when it opened its mouth to speak, the stench of rotten flesh and burnt hair overwhelmed his senses, forcing him to gag.

"Mom? Mommy? Wake up!" the Gamayun said in a young girl's trembling voice.

"What is it, baby?" it imitated a woman's reply.

"They are here, mom," the young girl continued. "I'm scared," she cried. "Are they going to eat us?"

"No, dear," the woman comforted. "Ael, Dad, and I will protect you. Here, take Kelpie and hide under the bed until we tell you—"

Screaming, slashing, scratching, more screaming, some thrashing. The Gamayun imitated every single noise with perfect clarity, making the rest of the party trade uncomfortable looks. Thuds of bodies falling, or of people running, then beastly growls and screeches followed by cries of children, of men and of women, as they met terribly violent deaths. Every noise down to the splashing of blood or the final breath leaving a person's chest, the Gamayun replicated perfectly. Then, it fell silent for a long moment, its nose still touching Daren's, its pupils swirling, and its hair dancing wildly.

A different crescendo began leaving the Gamayun's stinky mouth. It started with some low-volume growls, moans and grunts. Noises of slapping and slurping, followed by hard to distinguish whispers of fake comfort and forceful lust. It kept escalating in volume as the voices became more numerous and more violent, men and women, and children, all trapped in a hellish hurricane of pain and anguish as both virtue and dignity were being taken from them. The vocal indignities were then replaced by a different group of sounds, those of flesh ripping apart, cries of pain, and—

"ENOUGH! STOP!" Daren snapped in horror, breaking the Gamayun out of its trance. The creature startled, its face adapting a more humane expression. It jumped away from Daren's chest and quickly cuddled itself by the rocks it had been standing on earlier, shoving its head inside its wings, to everyone's stunned astonishment.

Anthia was the first to rush to Daren's side. "Are you alright?"

Daren brought himself to a sitting position with her help, breathing heavily. "What was *that?*"

"What were you thinking?!" Armon sneered.

"I-I didn't know what would happen..." Daren began to apologize.

"No, I didn't mean that," Armon corrected. "What were you *actually* thinking? When you touched the Gamayun, what was going through your mind?"

"Gamayun are prophetic creatures," Anthia explained, softly. "It is said that they can see into the future."

"Or the past," Master Sergeant Fran added, calmly. "You were thinking of Gierna, weren't you, boy?" He grimaced.

Daren squinted his eyes. "I'm not sure, I think..."

"I am so very sorry," a young woman's voice said, drawing everyone's attention to the Gamayun, peeking shily between its colorful wings. "I'm really sorry," it whimpered.

Stunned silence...

"By the Pale Towers," Master Sergeant Fran managed to murmur first.

"It's not supposed to be doing that, right?" Armon said, taking on a defensive stance, hands hovering over the handles of his curved blades.

"Who knows," shrugged Anthia. "Gamayun are very rare, we know very little about them."

"Please, don't hurt me, I didn't mean for it to happen," the Gamayun said before hiding its face in its feathers again.

"By the Pales, it did it again," Master Sergeant Fran said in disbelief. "It spoke."

Seeing as no one seemed interested in taking initiative, Daren rose to his feet, intending to approach the Gamayun. Anthia made a move to stop him but Daren gestured for her to trust him, and so did Master Sergeant Fran who seemed curious to see how Daren would handle the situation.

Daren kneeled before the colorful creature and using his still gloved, left hand, touched lightly on what he assumed could be considered its arm. The Gamayun, tensing on Daren's touch, seemed to be trembling. "Hey, little… b-bird? We are not going to hurt you, alright?"

The Gamayun peeked slowly between its wings, startling Daren. Its face was different now, similar features but more youthful than before, closer to Daren's age, and it had also grown… *nipples? Is it trying to appeal to me?* Daren thought, suspicious. Fae creatures were known to be manipulative and seductive. He brought his right, ungloved hand behind his back and formed three signs with his fingers. At that signal, the other three Binders set their hands on their weapons and subtly started moving closer.

"Do you promise?" the Gamayun asked, an invisible breeze rustling its hair backward, revealing more of its beautiful face.

"I-um," Daren faltered. "Yes, I promise," he nodded. The Gamayun's voice was perplexing. Not only was it crisp and clear, but its sentences were also perfectly coherent.

The Gamayun slowly lowered its wings. "Thank you," it said. "You are nice." It smiled prettily, a child's smile.

Daren was taken aback by the sincerity of its—*her* smile. He opened his right palm, signaling that there was no danger and settled down more comfortably, on one knee. "Do you... have a name?"

"Name?" the Gamayun echoed, seemingly confused. She cocked her head with a characteristically sudden movement, akin to that of a bird. "Oh, name! Yes! I do have a name!" she said, hopping excitedly. "You are so nice! No one has ever asked for my name before... or has talked to me, I think?" she trailed off, muttering something to herself.

Daren looked at his companions, baffled, but received shrugs in return. "So, what is it?" he asked the Gamayun.

"What? Oh, my name! Yara! Yara, it's Yara!" She cleared her throat and offered a surprisingly elegant curtsey, with her wings pointed upward and forehead almost touching the ground, though her hair danced about as if rustled by a strong breeze, yet never touching the soil. "My name is Yara," she repeated in a more composed manner.

Daren blinked a few times. Swallowed. "Ni-nice to meet you, Yara. My name is Daren," he said, offering his gloved hand. Yara snapped forward, and using the flexibility of a neck that could only have belonged to a bird, looked at Daren's hand curiously—from all directions. Then she set her forehead on his palm. Daren chuckled, as did Anthia. The other two Binders, whose expressions were more analogous to those of confusion, did not look as entertained.

Daren introduced the rest of the party to Yara and she offered the same, elegant curtsey to them as she had done for Daren. She did so pointedly, in descending order of age, starting from Master Sergeant Fran, to Armon, and lastly to Anthia. It seemed like etiquette was important to her on a fundamental level, though, unsurprisingly, she was unfamiliar with handshakes.

"Is it just me or does she look different?" Armon whispered to Anthia, using a hand to cover his mouth.

Anthia leaned closer to Armon. "You mean the bobbles, don't you?" she whispered back.

"So, Yara, right?" Master Sergeant Fran inquired. "Can you tell us about what you saw earlier, in your vision?"

"Hm?" Yara perked, inquisitively, her avian legs shaking excitedly.

"The vision," the old Binder explained. "Can you tell us about it?"

"Vision?" Yara froze, her eyes watering instantly. "No, please don't hurt me!" she cried, shoving her head inside her wings again, whimpering. "I didn't want to see. I didn't mean to see, please!" Yara was begging like a young girl about to be scolded.

"Whoa, whoa there, kiddo," Master Sergeant Fran panicked, reaching for her. "No one is going to hurt you, you didn't do anything wrong. Right, Daren?" He gestured with his bushy eyebrows for support.

"Of course not," Daren said immediately.

"I didn't?" Yara said, peeking.

"No, you did not," Daren smiled at her. "It was just an accident."

Yara smiled with her sincere smile again. "Yes, it was an accident. I didn't want to look at the threads, that makes it an accident, right?" Her smile widened, revealing pearly teeth. "I didn't mean to do it, so it was an accident!" She confirmed excitedly, mostly to herself.

Daren glanced at the old Binder who nodded. Armon's and Anthia's attention was also drawn to Daren's interaction, as they broke free of the silly and vulgar whispering about Yara's anatomy that they had engaged themselves into.

Daren paused for a short moment, considering how to approach this. "It must be incredible, Yara," he finally said. "Being able to see at the… threads."

"It is?"

"Of course! No one else can do it, right?" Daren said, feigning child-like admiration. "You are special."

"Oh," Yara giggled, covering her mouth with a wing. "Thank you, you are special too," she returned the compliment.

Anthia leaned toward Armon. "Call me crazy if you want but I think that bird is hitting on our officer," she murmured.

"Me? Special? Nah." Daren waved a hand. "I can't see the threads as you do." He winked, though the gesture didn't seem to be familiar to her.

"Well, obviously, you are not like *me*," Yara said in a cocky tone that Daren thought adorable. "But your thread is very special," she added quickly. "I have never seen a thread changing color before. Well, I have, but not *this* color!"

"Threads have colors?"

Yara giggled again. "Of course, silly. Have you ever seen threads without color?"

Daren tilted his head. Yara's statement was… well, reasonable; everything had color. "So, if you've seen threads changing color before, what makes mine so special?" he asked, genuinely curious.

"It turns red!" Yara said, eyes wide with excitement. "I have never seen red thread before, but not only that. When it changes, it is also joined by two more red threads. Can you believe that?

Three red threads! One is light red, the thin one. *So very beautiful, but also so very lonely. The other one is a little darker and thicker, it looked to be stretching into eternity.*" She gestured by spreading her wings in a wide arc. "Beautiful too, but sad, and a little scary I think."

Daren looked to the Master Sergeant, then back to Yara. "Do you know what the red thread means, Yara?" he asked.

Yara smiled widely for a moment but then shook her head. "Yes, I've never seen it before."

Daren paused, trying to make sense of Yara's actions and words which seemed to contradict themselves. He chose to ignore her out-of-place smile and focused on her out-of-place words. "So, Yara—" She smiled again, giving Daren another pause. "Why are you smiling?"

"I like it," Yara said.

"You mean the red color?"

"No, my name." Yara teared up. "No one has called my name before," she sniffed, using her colorful wings to brush the tears.

Daren froze, unsure of how he was supposed to respond to this. Was she really getting emotional hearing her own name?

"Aww," Anthia sympathized. She quickly kneeled before Yara and reached tenderly toward her. "Such a beautiful name and no one has spoken it before?"

Yara nodded, large, teary eyes looking up at Anthia.

Daren rose to his feet, convinced it was wise to let Anthia handle this. "I don't think we can ask about the vision," he whispered to Master Sergeant Fran.

The old Binder nodded. "Agreed, she probably wasn't even aware of it when it happened." He looked to Daren. "I wouldn't ignore what she said about the threads though."

Daren agreed with a nod, looking back at Yara.

Anthia seemed to have a knack for getting Daren out of awkward situations. She had managed to engage the emotionally unstable creature in a conversation about beautiful words, of all things. Yara had a very unusual perspective on the subject. It looked like words for her were directly associated with colors. Her name, apparently, had a lot of green and blue in it, the colors of life.

"Fascinating, isn't it?" Master Sergeant Fran said. "I don't know about this whole color thing, but Gamayun are said to be able to see all aspects of time simultaneously. Past, present, and future, all at once. It's what makes them so mentally fickle."

Daren remained silent, observing the adorable exchange between Anthia and Yara. He couldn't help but feel sorry for the colorful creature over what it must've endured during the earlier trance. Daren wasn't sure how he could tell, but Yara seemed to be experiencing every moment of that vision, every stab wound, every hit or bite, the deprivation of virtue—she *lived* those things. He couldn't quite put his finger on it, but Daren knew that to be a fact. He shook his head. *Poor thing... he lamented. Those red threads though, what could they mean?* Master Sergeant Fran had advised against ignoring the Gamayun's words but that thought had never even crossed Daren's mind. He instinctively knew Yara's words to not be gibberish and was certain there was a meaning behind them. How he wished he could see the world through her eyes, if only for a little bit. A Fae creature that could see the entirety of time itself, it seemed unfathomable.

"Don't think too hard on it," Master Sergeant Fran said, having noticed Daren's contemplation.

Nodding, Daren picked the glove he had dropped earlier and put it on. He sighed, having a hard time taking his eyes off his palm. Sin Binder gloves were red, matching their single-sided, left pauldron and, in Daren's case, the stripe normally hanging behind his back, which he still had loosely wrapped around his neck. Why did those 'red threads' trouble him so? What was it about this creature that compelled him to heed its every word, even though he'd just met her?

"Some things, we are simply not meant to know," the old Binder said, meaningfully. He tapped Daren on the shoulder. "Time to get moving, Binders," he ordered. "Let's not forget why we are here, shall we?"

Leaning with his left shoulder on a protruding, towering rock, Daren stared at the ruins of Gierna that lay in the distance. On Master Sergeant Fran's order, the party had stopped for a breather.

They had settled upon a relatively flat boulder which was large enough to comfortably accommodate all party members. It was tipped at the edge and was elevated a few feet above the general mass of the surrounding terrain, offering a clear view of the ruined village.

Looking just below the edge of the boulder, there was a small clearing with a sole, large rock at the center. Daren noted that rock as being peculiar since it seemed to have been split in half by the tremendous force of a root vine that had made its way through it and had since then taken it in a thorny embrace.

From this spot, Daren could make out the individual wrecks of houses and trees of Gierna scaling up the hill, the image giving him a sense of melancholy. A lone, larger ruin seemed to be occupying the top of the village, a once-temple perhaps. Only a place of worship would have been this large. There was a lot of commotion coming from that area, half a dozen winged figures flying in circles above it. If Daren didn't know better, he would have assumed them to be hawks or falcons, patrolling their territory.

Harpies, clearly, had the same keen eyesight of their smaller relatives, as they had been aware of the Binders' presence for some time now. Their flock had become agitated, though Daren doubted they would attack before the Binders posed a direct threat to their nesting grounds. Still, he couldn't help but feel a sense of uneasiness envelop him. He knew it wasn't fear. Harpies, although dangerous, were not exactly formidable Chasmals. Could it be that he still felt unsettled by Yara's vision?

Master Sergeant Fran approached Daren, setting one foot on a rock beside him and leaning on his knee. "We are close. Half an hour at most," he said, nodding toward the ruins.

Daren turned to the old Binder, catching a glimpse of Yara from the corner of his eye. The peppy Gamayun was having a lively conversation with Armon and Anthia, spinning around in place and gesturing with her colorful wings. No one had objected when Yara asked if she could tag along, and she had been following the party in short, awkward hops since then. When Daren asked her why she wasn't flying instead, she had claimed that flying was too boring for her and that she would rather walk alongside her friends.

Yara seemed even younger now, no more than thirteen or fourteen years of age. Daren often caught glances of her ever-shifting features, and even though he hadn't managed to see it happen in real-time, there was no doubt about it, and the party had gotten accustomed to it by that point. Her height, hair, and general characteristics of her face remained the same, but her age seemed to be constantly shifting up and down, likely a reflection of her mood. *Such an interesting little thing,* Daren mused. The younger she looked, the more distinct the features of her face and exposed chest seemed, as if she was becoming ignorant of her own anatomy, less aware of social etiquette, just like a child would.

Observing her energetic interaction with Armon and Anthia, Daren found himself smiling. Another thing he had noticed about Yara, which seemed to have slipped by the others' attention, was the way she posed herself; she had been trying to treat her wings as hands, with mixed success, throwing her hair over her shoulder, thrusting her hip to the side when given the chance, and playfully shoving during conversations. Apparently, Yara had found Anthia's mannerisms just as enticing as Daren had, mimicking her quirky gestures to the best of her abilities. Seeing her act so clumsily feminine, was adorable. Yara wasn't just a Fae creature, she was a person, and a lovely one at that. Bizarre, and a bit embarrassing to look at, but lovely. *That vision though...* Daren's mind had kept slipping into contemplation over it—over its visceral nature. *What happened to you?* he wondered, looking back toward the ruined village.

"You are right, Sir," Daren addressed the old Binder. "When I touched Yara, I was thinking of Gierna."

Master Sergeant Fran nodded. "I suspected as much," he said, stroking at his mustache.

"What Yara saw..." Daren paused, recalling the agony his winged friend had conveyed during that spine-chilling vision. "It really happened, didn't it?"

"It would be a safe assumption, yes," the stocky man said with certainty. "Now, I'm no scholar and little is known about that gloomy period of history, but I was part of the expedition that discovered Gierna, some twenty years back, and the consensus is that Gierna was destroyed during the Blood Wars."

Daren frowned. *Vampires... Sinners,* he thought, disdainfully. The vilest of all Chasmal monsters and the real reason the order of the Sin Binders was formed.

As history had it; Blood Chasms were created by the Crimson Lords; powerful vampires who led their horde of vampire Thralls against humanity during the Blood Wars. Until one day when, with the help of a traitor, the Penta-Pantheon—the Archons of Illustrander—managed to raise the Pale Towers and bind themselves to them in order to cast the 'Edict of Dominance,' a one-of-a-kind spell which eradicated the vampire horde. But as Fae magic was never meant to be used for harm, and by going against that natural law, magic ceased to flow in mortal veins and eventually stopped being passed down through the generations. It was a high price to pay, but as a result, Illustrander was now encased by invisible barriers emitted from the Pale Towers that protected the capital and its surrounding provinces from Chasmals, effectively making the Basin of Aellus, the safest and most stable place in the world. Where the Pale Towers couldn't reach—the Sin Binders did.

Admittedly, the whole part about the Pale Towers being raised in an instant seemed a bit… excessive, but—

Daren tensed, breaking out of his train of thought. Eyes wide, he looked back to Yara. *The red threads!* He slowly turned toward Master Sergeant Fran, and upon witnessing the slow shake of his head, Daren knew immediately that the old Binder had come to that conclusion much earlier than he had.

"Some things, we are simply not meant to know," the old Binder quoted himself, in a low voice.

Daren threw his back on the towering rock he'd been leaning on and let himself slide to the ground. "What am I supposed to do with this not-meant-to-have knowledge?" he asked, though he didn't know why.

"Weave it," the old Binder answered immediately. "Bend it to your will, or…" He shrugged. "Ignore it. After all, it was a funny-looking chicken that told you about it." He smiled, gesturing for Daren to get up.

Daren grinned, shaking his head in disbelief. *How gullible could I be?* He thought. *How is it possible that I was seized with despair at the mere idea of a vague and foolish prophecy? 'Red threads…'* he reminded himself. *Vampires eh? Hmph! So be it!* he mocked silently and looked up at the old man. "Good point," he said, laughingly, and rose to his feet with renewed confidence.

***

The transition from wilderness to the ruins of the village was hardly noticeable. The first few buildings of Gierna had been hit hard by nature's neverending lust for growth, most likely due to the relatively low elevation which offered more favorable conditions for plant life to grow and claim, while the harsh rock formations and tall trees protected the area from winds and dryness. Scaling up the hill though, most of the buildings were in relatively good condition, except for that large ruin of the temple at the top. The first stand-out feature of Gierna was a flat, octagonal area of weathered gravel that seemed to have served as the town's square, with some sort of circular, wooden construct still standing at its center. Although there were no visible pathways around the settlement, things on the inside were different. Numerous paths sprang from the octagonal plaza, mirroring its gravel, and spread from house to house throughout the entire hill, reuniting at the top where the temple used to be.

Making his way toward the wooden structure, Daren tried to imagine what Gierna might have looked like once. He imagined it as a place bustling with life and activity, this very square being used for the various festivities that would have taken place, perhaps harvest festivals, so commonly seen in the outskirts of Illustrander, or religious celebrations. A wonder, if he could hazard a guess.

"Cute," Anthia said, approaching Daren from behind.

"Hm? What is?" Daren asked, turning to her.

"You," she said. "That look of wonder on your face." She smiled. "What's so fascinating about these old rocks? Having lived in Illustrander, surely, this is nothing to gawk at."

"Illustrander is overrated, didn't you say so yourself?"

"Yeah," she giggled, "I guess, I did."

"It's not about the rocks," Daren said, kneeling to inspect the round, wooden structure. "It's about the stories they would tell if given a voice." It seemed to be the foundations of a platform, a dancing floor maybe.

Anthia crouched by Daren's left side, cheek on her knees and forearms, looking at him. "So, what does it say?" she asked jokingly, pointing with her delicate, dark eyebrows toward the wood.

Daren opened his mouth to retort but realized that Yara had just crouched on his other side too, copying Anthia's pose as faithfully as her avian legs allowed. *Her* expression, however, was the exact opposite of Anthia's.

"Sad, isn't it?" Yara asked, eyes blurry.

With the characteristic speed of a Fencer, Anthia rushed to Yara in an instant and wrapped her arms around her. "Aww, why are you crying, pretty?" The two had gotten very close, and Daren had found their rapidly growing relationship to be very charming.

"So many beautiful threads—torn apart," Yara whimpered, her voice muffled by her colorful wings pressed against her mouth due to Anthia's tight hug.

"Oh, don't be sad. Bad things happen sometimes," Anthia comforted, stroking Yara's hair. She looked up to Daren and shrugged discreetly.

Daren found himself smiling, though he wasn't sure whether it was Anthia's motherly tenderness or Yara's good-natured candidness that had enchanted him so.

"It used to be a staging terrace," Master Sergeant Fran said. "Though, it looked like a mass grave when we first discovered it."

Daren turned to the old man.

He grimaced, crossing his large hands. "Believe it or not, it wasn't desuetude that destroyed it, but us, Binders. You see, the condition these remains were in, what little was left of them anyway, had suggested gruesome, inhumane deaths. The Officer in charge of the expedition was so appalled by the discovery that she ordered us to burn them alongside the rest we had found." He nodded toward the remnants of a larger building to the left of the plaza. It was now overgrown but the signs of fire were evident on its churned remains. "We used the wood of the terrace for the pyre. May their poor souls find their way into Moira's Realm of Fae." The old Binder saluted reverently with a fist on his leather pauldron.

"Sad, indeed," Daren whispered solemnly, looking back to Yara.

"Well, will you look at that," Armon joined in, abruptly. "Here comes our welcome committee."

***

Bestiaries always described harpies as avian hybrids with a woman's head and torso, but if what Daren had before him was of any indication, the authors had been generous with their descriptions.

Three of the horrible birds had landed a few feet away from the party. He had expected something akin to the little Gamayun that was cuddling with Anthia by his feet, but they lacked everything that made Yara the magnificent creature that she was. They were slightly smaller than her, with feathers in the shades of grays and browns, as opposed to Yara's vibrant blues, reds, and yellows. Whatever skin was exposed looked like that of a plucked chicken, spotty and dotted with harsh hairs. Their mouths were in the shape of badly formed beaks, and their avian eyes were located deep within the skull sockets of their browless faces, giving them a very unsettling, monstrous outlook.

At least they got the smell right, Daren ridiculed, pulling the stripe around his neck over his mouth with one hand. Even at this distance, the stench of dead flesh and manure was overwhelming.

Anthia rose slowly, one hand on the handle of her rapier, the other lightly shoving Yara behind her.

"Hold on, let's see what they do," Armon said.

"I'm not sure I wanna risk it," Anthia said, leaning, with her right foot slowly sliding forward.

"They won't attack, we are not a threat yet," Master Sergeant Fran assured. "They only want to warn us that this is their territory."

Daren noticed that all his fellow Binders had reached for their weapons, an instinct that he had yet to cultivate.

Suddenly, Yara took flight and landed just before the three harpies.

Anthia gasped, tensing visibly.

"Hold positions!" the Master Sergeant ordered. "Let's see what happens."

Yara lowered her head to the ground, and raised her wings, offering her familiar, elegant curtsey.

The harpy standing closest to Yara leaned forward slowly, its head adapting a predatory position low, over the chest, and leaped, taloned feet lurching directly for Yara's head.

Daren didn't even have time to reach for his sword when the harpy's head flew in the air. As a fencer, Anthia's movements were precise and explosive. She had surged forward with a swift cut that had severed the monster's head from its body in an instant.

"NO! Why did you do that?!" Yara shouted.

Yara's voice distracted Anthia which led to one of the other harpies lurching for her instead. It managed a deep scratch on Anthia's neck before it was met with Armon's thrown sword, which took the creature somewhere in the chest and drove it backward.

The third harpy attacked Armon. He blocked its talons with his second sword, then grabbed it by one wing and threw it to the ground, where it found itself under the glistering edge of Master Sergeant Fran's greataxe.

It was all over in an instant and Daren hadn't even drawn his weapon yet.

A powerful scream came from the second harpy that lay on the ground with Armon's sword still stuck in its chest. Anthia rushed to it and stepped on the weapon, driving it in deeper, as well as stabbing her rapier through the harpy's throat, ending its life.

Armon cursed under his breath.

The dozen or so harpies that were flying above the ruined temple started screaming frantically, many more of the monsters joining them in the air.

"Get ready Binders, this is gonna get ugly!" Master Sergeant Fran called. Looking up, he gasped. "By the Pale Towers…" he murmured, eyes wide.

One more figure ascended from the ground, joining the commotion of the harpies which made way for it to poise among them. Its gigantic wings only needed to flap twice to bring it at the epicenter of the screaming birds. This figure was large and imposing, twice the size of a fully-grown horse, with the body, back legs, and tail comparable to those of a lion. In contrast to the unsightly and awkward flutter of the harpies surrounding it, this creature hovered with elegance and precision, its head and wings resembling those of an eagle.

Daren gawked, trying to wrap his mind around what he had been witnessing.

"Well, shit," Armon cursed. "A gryphon."

✳✳✳

The gryphon let out a deafening screech that overshadowed the combination of the two dozen of harpies screaming around it. With one more flap of its wings, it soared, brought its wings to close together, and started rapidly descending upon the Binders, taloned legs forward.

"TAKE COVER!" Master Sergeant Fran shouted as he threw himself backward.

Daren broke out of his shock and followed the old Binder's example.

Anthia pulled Armon's sword from the corpse of the harpy before her and threw it over to him as he ran toward the nearest building.

Rushing to grab Yara who seemed utterly confused by the situation, Anthia just barely managed to roll out of the way with the colorful bird in her arms, when the gryphon landed on the wooden terrace, demolishing it to splinters. The shockwave of the impact threw all four Binders off their feet.

The gryphon stood and spun about, facing away from Daren and toward Anthia and Armon, with the old Binder further down to Daren's left, effectively splitting the group in half. It stood tall on four intimidating legs and had an elegance to its pose that, even under these circumstances, was difficult to ignore. Its feline fur was white but harsh-looking, with each hair resembling an oversized needle. Its frontal part, that of an eagle, was covered with dark-colored feathers, streaked by golden stripes.

Glancing back momentarily, the gryphon swung its long tail toward the old Binder who managed to use his greataxe to block the attack, but the power of the swing was tremendous even for a man of his size, sending him crashing against the nearest wall and losing consciousness. It then made its way to Daren, though he managed to duck under it and roll away.

Daren came to a crouching position, with one knee and a hand touching the ground, the other hand making for his sword—a stance that was very familiar to him from his training. He stayed in that pose, expecting the next swing of the gryphon's tail which never came. The gryphon rushed forward, aiming for where Anthia and Yara seemed to be located. Daren's first instinct was to immediately rush to their aid, but he couldn't ignore the several harpies that had started descending upon the old Binder's unconscious body.

Daren cursed, dashing toward the Master Sergeant. Upon nearing, he leaped with a two-handed, upward swing that found the first harpy to arrive on the belly. To his surprise, his slash didn't cut that deep into the monster, though it *did* disable it. Two more harpies arrived and Daren fended them off with more slashes. More and more kept showing up, one after the other—a chaotic bewilderment of screams and scratches. It reached a point where it had become impossible to keep track of their numbers. It was the first time in Daren's life that his blade had been going through real flesh and his cuts were meeting far more resistance than he had ever anticipated, with each swing rapidly becoming heavier than the previous one.

The harpies kept trying to get a hold of Daren in whatever manner they could, their talons often digging deep into his shoulders and hands. They would have ripped him apart by now if it wasn't for the sturdy material of the Sin Binder's uniform that had kept them in a challenge.

Daren kept swinging his sword frantically, almost blindly, shielding his eyes. His desperate slashes sometimes found targets, sometimes did not—adding to his fatigue. It was fruitless, and all he could do against their numbers was to crouch on the ground and protect his head as the filthy birds kept poking and pulling at him. *Stay down, stay down, stay...* "'down, low on the floor,'" Daren quoted one of his trainers from the academy. "'The floor is your domain, the floor is your *playground*,'" he recalled. Anger lit a slumbered flame inside him, "and you are nothing but *pests!*" he sneered, bringing himself on one knee, and swinging his sword in a wide arc over his head, clearing the immediate area around him. Then, staying in that stance, he darted his eyes around, making note of the nearest *pest*. He slashed downward, shifting from knee to knee which matched and empowered the swing accordingly. For the first time, his blade cut cleanly, severing the pest in two. Daren's next attacks were just as efficient, with five more cuts killing an equal amount of harpies. When the sixth pest's turn came, a dagger flew just above Daren's head, taking the bird right in the face.

Master Sergeant Fran had finally regained consciousness. "Go!" he ordered immediately. "See if you can help the others!" He rose, using his greataxe to steady himself.

"What about you?"

The old Binder undid the golden chain from his shoulder with a well-practiced flourish and threw it, catching a harpy mid-air by the neck as it was about to lurch for Daren. He dragged it to him and stomped its head flat, with a disgusting, crunching sound that made Daren wince. "GO!" He pointed toward the gryphon which seemed to have given chase among the ruins.

Daren nodded. There was no time for second-guessing or doubt. He dashed toward the gryphon, cutting one more harpy down on his way there. Once his feet felt the weathered gravel of the town's square, Daren glanced backward, which told him that, despite his injuries, Master Sergeant Fran was at least twice as strong as he was. Daren saw the old Binder taking down a harpy with his bare hands and then slamming it with his greataxe, for good measure. Unfortunately, the situation was much different for the other two Binders.

The gryphon was slowly progressing further into the ruined village, running its massive body through everything that stood in its way. The old structures, too weathered down by the passage of time, didn't seem to offer much resistance to its persistent rampaging.

Daren stopped abruptly, upon witnessing the destruction. What could *he* do against such a massive beast?

The answer came in the form of Armon, leaping off of a building, twin blades held high. He had managed a few good cuts on the monster already, and had even climbed on its back for a brief moment, but with each strike he'd dealt, the gryphon had simply turned around with feline agility and fended him off, before immediately returning to its chase.

Seeing Armon's impressive maneuvers, something stirred inside Daren. The gryphon suddenly seemed smaller, though not by much, and he could now see ways in which he could fight it.

It seemed stubbornly focused on Anthia, no, not Anthia, but the colorful creature in her arms. Chasmals, monsters that originate from Blood Chasms, had an inherited hatred for Fae creatures. Undeterred in its single-minded desire to capture its prey, the gryphon was after *Yara.*

Armon went for another attack, jumping from the elevated courtyard of a ruined house, in an attempt to climb on the gryphon's back again, but was met mid-air with the strong swing of its tail, sending him crashing awkwardly.

Daren dashed to him and slid by his side. "You alright?"

Armon grunted, rubbing his left arm. "Anthia is holed up in that building with Yara." He gestured toward the gryphon which seemed to be trying to reach its talons somewhere deep inside a smaller room. "I haven't managed to draw its attention, my blades are too light to penetrate its mane. Where's the old man? We could use his axe."

Daren looked down at his longsword. "Mine should do the trick."

Armon looked at the sword. "It might," he nodded, and tried to get back on his feet but immediately succumbed under his own weight. "Fuck!"

"Don't move, I think you have a broken leg."

"Shit!" Armon looked around frantically. "Try to draw the gryphon in there." He pointed toward a narrow passage between the buildings. "It will give you a fighting chance."

Daren nodded, turning to face the gryphon. It was screeching and scratching furiously, trying to reach inside the house. Keeping a fifteen feet distance from it, just out of reach of its tail which wiped left and right, Daren started circling the monster, looking for an opening. In order to draw the gryphon's attention, his attack needed to cause real damage, otherwise, he would simply be ignored, just like Armon had been earlier, and

Daren couldn't afford to drag the fight for much longer. He was already winded out, with both Armon and Master Sergeant Fran having been injured. No, Daren had to do this right, he had to force the beast to follow him, he had to bring the fight to his own… 'playground.'

The combination of recklessly going through buildings and Armon's attacks had left the gryphon with several wounds all over its body, with one, in particular, drawing Daren's attention. It was a deep cut near the base of its tail, *that's* what he had to go for. A simple cut on its tail wouldn't do the trick, for it was too thick for any sword to penetrate, but if Daren aimed for that already weakened spot, it was bound to at least draw the monster's attention. He had already witnessed the deadly appendage in action twice—it was time for it to go.

Still out of reach, Daren tightened the stripe around his mouth and lowered his body to the ground, left knee and hand touching down, his silvery longsword extended to the side. He took a deep breath, "my playground," he whispered and dashed forward. He dropped and slid from knee to knee, as he evaded each blind whip of the deadly tail. Upon reaching his targeted area, he curled upward, in a clockwise twist, bringing his sword in a wide arc around himself and, with his entire weight assisting, slashed downward in a powerful, two-handed grip.

The gryphon let out a thunderous screech that forced Daren to cover his ears. It stomped furiously and kicked with its hind legs. Daren rolled away from both the beast and his weapon, which remained stuck on the gryphon's tail. The gryphon kept stomping and spinning around itself, trying to reach for its tail but unable to. After a few more unsuccessful attempts, it opened its massive wings wide, flapped once, rising high in the air, then let itself drop. The violent crash got the sword unstuck at the cost of its tail. which fell on the ground, spasming. The gryphon slammed its front legs a few more times but eventually calmed down, and, fixing its avian eyes on Daren, set one taloned foot forward and lowered its body, prepared to charge.

Daren started stepping backward, slowly. "Guess I got your attention now." He tilted his head slightly, looking at his longsword that had remained on the other side of the massive beast. "Lucky me." He fingered the golden chain that hung on his armband with one hand, and reached behind him for the dagger attached to his belt—both useless against such a beast, but they did offer some false sense of—

"The alley!" Armon shouted, from the building he had climbed for cover.

Not sparing it a second thought, Daren spun about and started running with all his might, the gryphon immediately pouncing on his trail.

Armon threw one of his curved blades Daren's way, who caught it in mid-air as it bounced off the gravel. With the sword now in hand, Daren entered the narrow passage, large enough to accommodate a single person but not enough to deter the gryphon from ramming through the rock buildings and wooden columns that supported their balconies, quickly catching up to him.

Unable to outpace the beast, Daren slid to a crouched position and turned, swinging. The gryphon didn't even flinch from his attacks and Daren was soon forced to use Armon's sword to stop the gryphon's beak from penetrating him, its attack throwing him on his back. Thankfully, the restrictive surroundings didn't allow the gryphon to bring forth its taloned legs. He held the sword with both hands across its gaping, beaked mouth, as it was trying to tilt around and reach for his flesh. Daren screamed against the strain of the gryphon's force, pushing him through the dirt, the gravel rubbing against the back of his head and neck.

The bloodlust in the gryphon's avian eyes was terrifying, its stinking breath, choking Daren as he desperately tried to suck in much-needed air. Daren screamed and kicked, trying to avert the continuous thrust to the side—but to no avail. "It won't end like this!" he sneered between teeth, his bloodshot, green eyes locked with the beast's vicious yellow. His elbows buckled, and Daren screamed louder, pushing with all his might. He managed to force the beast back, the edge of Armon's blade drawing blood from the hinges of its beak, though the wounds didn't seem enough to hinder it.

After a long, agonizing moment of rage and strain as the strength in his arms seeped away, Daren thought with unexpected serenity: *Looks like this is the end of the line for me...* Somehow, he found himself smiling at the thought. *And I had just started getting acquainted with this whole 'freedom' thing that Anthia seemed so passionate about.* He grinned, defiantly looking the gryphon in the eyes, and as his grip started loosening—

A shadow, a familiar, slender figure, jumped from behind the gryphon and landed on its back, ramming the beast right through the neck with a longsword; *Daren's* longsword.

Anthia rolled over right after, scurrying next to Daren. Once there, she pulled her rapier out and stabbed the beast in the eye. Shocked by the realization that the gryphon was unfazed by both injuries, Anthia tried to go for a second stab, but the violent jerking of the gryphon's head made it impossible for her to get a good grip on the rapier's hilt. With Daren's hands starting to buckle under the stress, Anthia rushed to lay alongside him, using her booted feet on Armon's sword to support Daren's hold against the gryphon's fierce, final struggle.

After what must have been two, long, agonizing minutes of united exertion, the gryphon finally fell silent, its good eye rolling upward and its body going limp. Its final, stinky breath left its massive body in a long, sickly hiss.

Daren pushed the gryphon's lifeless head to the side and Anthia, after having assisted the push with her foot, let her leg drop across Daren's chest. Both continued to lay down, breathing heavily.

"Are we alive?" Anthia asked.

Daren tapped her leg with his left hand. "I think we just brought down an Alpha Chasmal," he chuckled.

Anthia brought her upper body over, slowly, took Daren's head in her hands, and set her forehead on his, her sweat-drenched braids, falling on his face. "Back in that, dark room… I thought I was a goner," she whispered, tearing up. "Thank you," she wept, her voice breaking. "Thank you for saving me, Daren."

Daren moved his hand from her leg to her dark hair. "So did you, Anthia," he said, smiling.

They locked eyes and remained like that for a long, savored moment. Anthia's scent of sweat and dirt was an incredibly refreshing change from the gryphon's stink of rot and death. "We should go check on the others," Daren finally said, rubbing the tears from her cheek.

Anthia nodded, her beautiful face streaked by muddy tears which gathered in the crevice under her trembling, lower lip. "Let's."

***

After having recovered their weapons from the gryphon's corpse, the first person Daren and Anthia met was Armon, who had come down from the ruined house he'd climbed and was in the process of setting an improvised splint for his leg. Anthia rushed over to check on his injuries.

"I'm fine," Armon said, raising a hand. "It's not broken. Just a sprain."

Anthia felt for Armon's leg. "Seems about right," she confirmed.

"Thanks for the assist earlier," Daren said, returning Armon's sword. "I would have been dead if it wasn't for you."

Armon nodded, and looking down the path, he grinned. "Looks like the old man made it too."

Limping slightly, Master Sergeant Fran was making his way to them, greataxe resting comfortably on his left shoulder, the other hand rubbing his ribs. As he was passing by, he nodded toward the gryphon's corpse lying to his right. "Good work with that one," he said, nonchalantly.

"Took you long enough," Armon smirked.

"Bah!" the old Binder exclaimed as he let his greataxe drop and set his hands on it. "I would've loved to see how you'd fare once you entered the sixth decade of your life." He shook his head. "I'm too old for this." Then, sweeping his dark, weary eyes across them, he burst laughing, heartily. "Taking down an Alpha Chasmal, and a gryphon at that… you are only the second group to have achieved that in many decades. Few can claim such a feat, *very* few. Such feats are usually attributed to the 'Bloodstained.'" He nodded approvingly, his expression suggesting both pride and relief. "Well done, kids. Truly remarkable work. All three of you are now eligible for a promotion, and the medal of Chasmal Slayers."

The three, younger Binders exchanged looks, with only Armon not looking surprised.

"We now know what forced the harpies to such radical behavior," Daren noted, matter-of-factly, in an attempt to hide his unprofessional pride.

"Indeed," Master Sergeant Fran said. "Alpha Chasmals can compel lesser Chasmals, like harpies, to do their bidding. That gryphon had been enjoying free meals for a while now."

"Why here?" Armon asked. "Why was an Alpha here?"

Master Sergeant Fran stroked at his mustache. "Alphas may be more common around Blood Chasms, but that doesn't mean they are restrained by them. Not as far as we know anyway," he explained at length.

Armon didn't seem pleased by the explanation but rather contemplative.

"What's our next move, Sir?" Daren inquired.

Master Sergeant Fran looked at the sun's position. "It's past midday," he noted, idly. "I wanted us to take a closer look at the nesting grounds but I think we can all agree that the threat has been neutralized. We will tend to our wounds and rest for a bit, but we must make it back to the horses by dusk. I don't want us to risk any infections. It would have been a right pity to defeat an Alpha Chasmal, only to be taken down by fevers and chills. Also, I want you to..." he trailed off, looking around. "Where is Yara?"

Anthia lowered her head.

Armon looked up to her with a solemn expression. "Yara is still in there," he said, pointing toward the building where Anthia and Yara had taken refuge earlier. "She… doesn't seem right."

"I'll… go check on her," Anthia said and staggered inside.

"What's wrong with Yara? Is she injured?" Daren asked, offering his hand.

Armon accepted Daren's hand and rose to his feet "No, but…" He grimaced. "Let's go in, you'll see."

Yara was murmuring something unintelligible while throwing her head around in erratic, random patterns. Daren couldn't be certain, but it seemed like she was in many places at the same time, each spasmodic movement of her head directing her attention to a different event. She appeared to be in a state of mind that couldn't distinguish between past, present or future. It was the same as when Master Sergeant Fran had explained the Gamayun's nature. Yara looked older now. Her face had returned to that of a beautiful woman in her mid-twenties, with withheld chest features and porcelain skin that moved without elasticity.

Anthia removed her gloves and, hesitantly, reached for the little Gamayun in hopes of breaking her out of the trance. Nothing happened.

"Anthia." Armon set a hand on her shoulder. "We should go. I don't know if there's anything that we can do here," he said, squeezing.

"There isn't," Master Sergeant Fran said, calmly. "For there is nothing wrong with her. She is simply back to her normal self. Take joy in the fact that she is uninjured."

Anthia nodded slowly. "Just, give me a moment, please."

"Alright, but don't take too long, we should have that cut on your neck checked too," the Master Sergeant said. "We'll be waiting at the town's square."

Limbing by Daren, Armon elbowed him lightly and nodded toward the rocky path.

"Go on ahead," Daren said.

Anthia sniffed, stroking Yara's cheeks and wavering hair. Daren kneeled beside her. "I'll miss her too."

"It's my fault, isn't it?" Anthia sobbed. "When I killed that first harpy."

"What? No, don't do that," Daren hurried a reply. "Don't beat yourself over something like that. You saved her life, Anthia."

"But maybe, I could—"

"Cut it out," Daren interrupted her stuttering, a bit more rudely than he had intended. "She wouldn't have been able to follow us for much longer. We would eventually have reached the barriers of the Pale Towers, and Fae creatures cannot cross past that point." He grimaced. The Pale Towers were supposed to protect from Chasmals, not from Fae. Yet, somehow, the barriers affected both. "It was inevitable," he said, in a lower voice.

"I know. I know, I just… I just wished we could have parted ways more appropriately."

Daren studied Anthia for a short moment. "We don't really know how her mind works," he reminded her. "Something tells me that you haven't missed your chance to say goodbye yet. She may not be fully aware of it at the moment, but I think it will stay with her regardless." He nodded confidently to himself. "Yeah, I have no doubt about it."

Anthia nodded and stretched her arms to take Yara into a tight hug. Daren knew that Anthia couldn't see it, but Yara's eyes seemed focused during the gesture. "Goodbye, pretty," she said, settling back on her knees. She rubbed her teary eyes with her palms before rising and plodding away, her gloves clenched tightly in one hand.

Daren looked to Yara who seemed to be in that trance-like state as when they had first met her. Did he imagine her eyes focusing earlier? He frowned, and after making sure that Anthia wasn't looking, he removed his right glove and set his hand on Yara's cheek, which, to his surprise, was actually soft and warm to the touch. He started. "Yara?"

Yara nodded.

"By the Pales, why didn't you say something?" Daren wrapped his arms around her small figure, a gesture that surprised even himself. When had he grown so attached to the little bird?

He turned, intending to call to Anthia, but Yara used her colorful wing to obscure his view.

"It's better this way," she said, in a very mature and composed manner.

Daren turned from Anthia's distancing figure back to Yara. "I don't understand, why?"

"My mothers wouldn't allow it, you have to trust me."

'Mothers?' Daren nodded. Something deep inside warned him to heed the Gamayun's words. "She will miss you, you know."

"I know, I will miss her too."

"What will you do now?"

"I have my own calling, just like you have yours."

"My… calling?" Daren asked, settling back. His mind slid back to the Pledge Bearers, but it was too early for that, wasn't it?

"I cannot speak about it directly, but I can offer you advice," Yara said in such a mature tone that Daren found it disturbing.

"I'm listening."

"The red threads, Daren. When the time comes, embrace them—let them entwine. Let them twist and interweave on the tapestry of time."

"I'm not sure, I…" Daren trailed off.

"Just promise me that you will, Daren," Yara prodded. "I'm sorry I cannot be more direct, but trust me, Daren, it is imperative that you do."

Daren swallowed nervously. *'Embrace the red threads…'* He couldn't decide what to make of this information, but knew instinctively that further questioning would prove fruitless, and, in some unusual manner, Yara's directive offered him consolation. He nodded. "Thank you, Yara. I promise," he said, standing to his feet. Yara nodded back, and the fact that she didn't smile upon hearing her name made Daren feel an uncalled-for nostalgia. Was that energetic, young kid under Yara's guise gone forever? "Will we—"

"We will," Yara cut him off. She offered Daren her elegant curtsey one last time, head low on the ground and wings stretched upward. "We will meet again, Daren Sailseeth," she said with an incredibly honest smile—a child's smile—painted across her beautiful face.

Daren bit at his lower lip, he wasn't even surprised that she knew his full name. He bowed deeply before the little Gamayun. "Take care of yourself," he said, smiling back, and turned around.

Looking one last time over his shoulder, he couldn't help but add, "you really *are* special, Yara."

Yara giggled prettily. "So are you, Daren."

Coming out of the ruin, Daren was met with the pleasantly cool breeze of the mountain which replaced the stench—if only momentarily—of his clothing. Chasmals really *did* stink, and he had their blood, and other, nastier stuff, all over him. He checked his extremities for possible injuries. Somehow, there were none, except for a few minor scratches and bruises on his back. The weariness that had been tormenting him had finally left his body, and a sense of accomplishment and joy took its place. This was his first contract, his first *real* day of active duty. His first time of using his weapon for something other than teasing wooden dummies. His first time fighting, speaking, and even befriending mythical creatures that he'd only known from book depictions. His first time outside the great granite walls of Illustrander. His first time understanding… *freedom.*

It was silent, save for the whistling of the wind through crevices and old windows. Daren took a deep breath and nodded to himself, contentedly.

It was a good day.

***

As Daren had anticipated, the promotion ceremony was nothing spectacular. It would probably have been more sentimental if he had a family to accompany him, but alas, it consisted of him standing alone among an endless sea of intricate metalwork which served as decoration, in a large, circular room made of marble—like all rooms were inside the Western Pale Tower—surrounded by high ranking Sin Binders and giving oaths of fealty and servitude. It *was* a military celebration after all. Soldiers were not supposed to express feelings in any form, not in the presence of officials anyway. Instead, they were limited to saluting. Gratifying in its own right, but nothing compared to the cheers of raised tankards, songs, and laughs of the common folk which had celebrated Daren's success when his party handed over the completed contract at the townhall of Vilga, a small village at the foot of Karnerk Rise, and the place which had been hit the most by the harpy raids. It had been a week since then, only a week, yet to Daren, it felt like a lifetime ago.

Daren came out of the main gates of the Western Pale Tower, his departure followed by the sound of heavy plated hands slamming on sword guards. It was the salute of the two Paladins that stood guard. *Right, I'm an Officer now,* he thought with dulled excitement. He turned to the heavy armored Paladins and returned the gesture with his right fist on his left pauldron, which was now decorated by a golden-weaved, four-digit star, encased in a pattern mirroring the great walls of Illustrander as seen from above, marking him as a 'Second Lieutenant,' and a silver crest depicting a gryphon standing on its hind feet, proclaiming him a 'Chasmal Slayer.' *This will take some getting used to...*

Turning around, Daren found himself smiling. *She really* did *come.*

Further down the street which led inside the city of Illustrander, Anthia, dressed in her Sin Binder uniform of white and red, was leaning with her back and one booted foot against the marble of the Pale Tower, arms crossed. Upon noticing Daren's approach, she immediately composed herself and saluted, standing to attention.

"Really?" Daren smirked.

Anthia giggled, covering her mouth. "Well, you *are* a superior Officer now." She offered her hand. "Congratulations, Daren. You deserve it."

Daren accepted the handshake. "Thank you, Anthia." He let out an exasperated sigh. "Mighty above," he said, looking directly upward—*literally.* "You can't imagine how comforting it is to see a familiar face."

"Oh, don't be so overly dramatic, Daren. I'm sure all these old preachers in there are fun to hang around with, once you get to know them... and follow their rules without question, of course."

"You think so too?" Daren chuckled. "Yeah, I agree."

"So..." Anthia stepped closer to Daren and set her gloved hands on his uniform's collar, smoothing the edges. "Second Lieutenant now, eh?" she said, inspecting his leather pauldron. "It's been a while since I last saw an Officer's insignia up close. I had forgotten how incredibly intricate they were. Very beautiful handiwork." She looked Daren in the eyes. "It suits you."

Daren blushed, and although he had somehow managed to hold her gaze, not much else came from his effort. Why was it always so difficult to find words in her presence? He knew that he should have retorted by returning her compliment, he *knew* that, but all he'd managed to do was lose himself in her heartwarming, hazel eyes—almost golden now due to the sun's brilliant light, reflecting off of the Pale Tower's marble.

After having given him enough time for a compliment that was never returned. Anthia asked in a lowered voice. "Where did they station you?"

"I was sent to the Northern Pale Tower," Daren said, lowering his eyes. He'd hoped that he would be stationed here for a little longer. "It's standard procedure, I will serve there for about three years, then move East, and eventually, end up in the South Pale Tower. My true destination as an academy-grown officer."

Anthia nodded slowly. "How long will you be staying here?"

"Two weeks," Daren said, "off-duty, and… Um, I was hoping to find someone to show me around, you know, do some sightseeing and stuff."

Anthia's face brightened a bit. "Well then, in that case, two weeks is more than enough for me to show you around. I would much rather spend my time outside those suffocating walls of pretense, of course, but I will make an exception for you," she said, smiling. "See? I barely know you and I'm already making sacrifices for you." She poked him in the chest. "You better appreciate that, Sir."

"Noted," Daren chuckled and his eye caught Anthia's intricate weapon. "Um, while we're at it. Would you mind if I borrowed your sword?"

Anthia raised an eyebrow. "My rapier?" She looked down at her weapon and tapped it lightly. "Beautiful, isn't she?" she said, looking up into his eyes, conspicuously, her countenance betraying expectancy. Another pass for Daren to flirt with her, which he completely blundered—again.

She let out a resigned sigh. "It's a named sword, you know. It belonged to my mother."

"Really? Your mother is an Officer?"

"Was," she corrected. "A Captain. She's passed away." The hint of a grimace washed over her face.

"I'm sorry for your loss," Daren said, eyeing Anthia's medal of Chasmal Slayer. "She would have been proud of you," he added.

Anthia nodded, slowly. "Thank you," she said, looking down at her medal, and from there, to her weapon again. "This sword is the sole reason I ended up joining the order. My mother's parting gift—the greatest gift I have ever received. She passed it on to me on her deathbed, and it changed my life. I always suspected that she knew it would.

That's how mothers are, you know? They just… know things."

He didn't know. Daren had never known his mother, but he wouldn't allow this to bother him, not right now—not ever. There was a clear fondness in Anthia's low voice and Daren loved it, he loved seeing her wear such a heartfelt smile despite the small tears that had formed in her eyes. Fighting against his instincts to reach for her, to comfort her, Daren stayed firm and silent, having no intention of breaking Anthia out of her musings.

"Before that, I had nothing, I was nothing." She looked up to him. "I know, I know, I sound dramatic and all that but… I hadn't realized the freedom that came with being a Sin Binder. I used to think that Illustrander was all there is to it and it had never even crossed my mind to ever leave it behind. I was even considering getting married. Can you believe that?" She chuckled. "But this sword… It gave me purpose and direction. It taught me about the vastness, the *true* vastness of our beautiful world. Because it really *is* beautiful, Daren." She looked up at him, her hazel eyes flickering as they met Daren's green. "A vastness of which I was completely unaware." She blushed, breaking eye contact, and looking back down at the weapon. "It was this sword, my mother's sword, that taught me the true meaning of freedom," she paused, smiling to herself, the pretty redness of her cheeks retreating. "But that's a tale for another time. Isn't it?" She pulled out her rapier half-way, presenting it to Daren. "This is, Susperia. Named after my mother."

"Beautiful name."

"Really, Daren?" Anthia let Susperia slid back in its sheath and threw her hands to the sides in exaggerated disbelief. "I've been trying to squeeze a nice word out of you and when you finally do so, it's directed at my sword?"

"Wow, so blunt," Daren chuckled, scratching the back of his head. "Sorry, Anthia, I'm not very good with these things."

Anthia giggled. "It's fine, no worries. What do you want with it anyway?"

"Well, as an officer, I am now entitled to a named sword myself, and I'd like to order something using Susperia's crossguard."

"Hmm, a rapier crossguard on a longsword? How would that work?"

"Well," he shrugged, "it won't be a direct copy, but very similar to it. It's hard to explain, I'd have to show you."

"Oh, I see. And, have you come up with a name for it?"

"Yeah actually, I have…"

"So? What is it, tell me," Anthia urged.

Daren bit his lower lip and looked away. "Anthia," he said, shyly. "It's Anthia."

Anthia gaped and blinked rapidly a few times. "Finally!" she exclaimed.

Daren paused for a moment, before realizing. "Well, what do you know? An actual compliment." He nodded approvingly to himself.

"Not bad, if I do say so myself." He smiled, then took Anthia's hands into his own, and looked into her eyes. "Thank you, for saving my life, Anthia."

She chuckled. "So did you, Daren."

Daren nodded slowly. "So, shall we?" he said, presenting his elbow to her, a gentleman's gesture for his date to hold onto.

"Oh, how… polished of you," Anthia hesitated.

"Too much?" Daren asked, panicking.

"Nope." She excitedly wrapped her hands around his arm. "Perfect," she said, leaning her head on his shoulder.

Daren smiled, blushing even more, now that Anthia's warmth was so much more vivid. Thankfully, he had managed to suppress his excited trembling. "So, how are the others?"

"Oh, don't ruin the moment with that lot." She waved her left hand, dismissively. "Fran's injury was more serious than he'd let on, but he'll be fine; he should be up and running in a few weeks. And Armon, believe it or not, has already picked up a new contract and is headed back to Karnerk Rise—or so he said, anyway."

"You and Armon seem… close."

"Yup, he is a little older than me, but we grew up in the same neighborhood. We joined the order at the same time too."

"Back to Karnerk Rise, eh?" Daren mused. "He is difficult to like, but I got to give him credit, the guy's good. He had done a number on the gryphon way before I had gotten to it."

"He… has his reason for acting as he does. I'm sure he will find his footing, eventually."

"You seem to care dearly about him."

"Of course I do. We grew up together. Armon is like a brother to me, maybe more than that. I'm so used to his presence that it actually feels a little weird not having him around."

Daren nodded. "A tale for another time, I guess. So, shall we go to that place you said that overlooks the market District?"

"Yup, that we shall. Drinks on you, of course."

"Obviously, I'm the one celebrating after all."

Making their way out under the overarching marble of the Western Pale Tower, and stepping upon the pavement that indicated they were now inside the city of Illustrander, Anthia turned around, toward the west, and looked upward, above the granite walls, where the peak of Karnerk Rise protruded to the far distance. "Do you… think she will be safe?"

Daren followed Anthia's gaze and nodded. "Yeah, I believe so. In fact." He smiled, knowingly. "I am sure of it."

Epilogue

Armon stood before the mouth of the alley where the gryphon had left its last breath. Two harpies were feasting on its carcass. "The irony," he smirked.

Upon noticing him, both monsters turned sharply toward him, threateningly lowering their ugly heads in a predatory position.

"Don't be foolish," Armon said, impassively, crossing his arms. "I'm not here for you."

The harpies hissed and lurched for him. The first one was met with a thrown dagger in the face—dead before it had even spread its wings. The second harpy, Armon grabbed mid-air by the throat and threw on the ground, before crashing it with a booted foot on the back of its neck. He casually walked over the dumb monster's corpse and stood above the gryphon's—what little was left of it.

Smirking, he studied the half-eaten carcass, caring little for the stench. Thanks to this monster, Armon had now been promoted to a Sergeant, and the Chasmal Slayer medal that his uniform boasted had made him eligible for future officership. It would still take him over a decade to reach an officer's rank, but it was now a real prospect—he would get there, eventually.

Armon's moment of gloating didn't last long. As he let his eyes linger on the gryphon, his smirk turned into a frown. *Why would an Alpha Chasmal be here?* That question had tormented his nights for over a week now, ever since that fateful mission with Fran, Anthia, and that, unexpectedly competent trainee, Daren. The edge of his lips curved upward, recalling the young Officer. Daren seemed to be one of those individuals that were meant for positions of big import and responsibility amid the ranks of the Sin Binders. Despite his inexperience, he had stood his ground against a foe that would have made many cower in fear, saving Anthia's life in the process. Armon would always be grateful to Daren for saving his childhood friend.

When Armon had decided to join the Order of the Sin Binders, almost eight years earlier. Lady Susperia—Anthia's late mother—had entrusted him with watching over her daughter, even though, at the time, Anthia hadn't expressed any interest in joining up alongside him. It was as though Susperia knew exactly what her daughter would decide to do after her passing. Armon was eighteen years old at the time, with Anthia being three years younger.

He broke off from his contemplation, recalling the reason he'd returned to Karnerk Rise. He turned his head toward the west, the general direction of the temple ruins sitting at the top of the village—the harpies' nesting grounds.

Upon nearing the temple, Armon was overwhelmed by a familiar sense of dread that he hadn't felt in a long time. The murmur of raised voices and occasional rumbling of rocks suggested that he was not entirely alone. He hugged the walls of the last few houses before the temple and peeked from behind a corner.

Three figures stood by the wreck of marble, which was suspiciously similar to the marble of the Pale Towers. Armon gapped, eyes wide. He recognized all three; the young, handsome man on the left had dark skin and contrasting, blonde hair. Easily distinguishable by the six stripes of white and red that hung over his Sin Binder uniform, he was none other than High General Cornelius himself—the only man in the entirety of Illustrander carrying the rank of a high general. Next to him stood another, even more, imposing figure.

"By the Pale Towers," Armon whispered, awed.

The second man was of slightly shorter build than the High General, with matching hair and skin tones. He stood tall, hands clasped behind his back. His attire consisted mostly of black, rope-like fabrics with intricate, golden designs that wrapped around his body, a number of overlapping red stripes rippling on his back. Everyone could recognize that man, though very few had seen him in person. Even the basin that sheltered Illustrander was named after him. That man was the ruler of the Penta-Pantheon; High Archon Aellus Feomathdar—an actual *god*.

Armon hid again, his back touching the wall beside him. Why would the two most powerful men in the country, if not the world, be here? Could it be that Armon's suspicion about the gryphon's abnormal presence was correct? If so, what did that mean? He sighed heavily, peeking out again.

The third, much smaller, figure that stood in front of the two men, was Yara. She seemed distressed, waving her colorful wings in agitated movements. Was she in trouble? Armon shook his head. He knew he shouldn't intervene, but Anthia loved Yara, and Armon always trusted Anthia's instincts. With a heavy sigh, he decided against his better judgment and came out of his hiding spot.

The closer he got, the more dreadful he felt. Upon nearing, he caught part of what they were saying.

"—Please, don't do this," Yara was begging.

"For a spirit that can see into the future, you sure are persistent, aren't you?" High General Cornelius said. "I'm curious, truly. Why get in the way, when you already know the outcome?"

Yara eyed Armon and lowered her head. "I'm sorry, Armon," she said, voice small, as the two men turned to him.

Armon paused, he saluted the General and dropped to one knee in a respectful bow toward the High Archon.

The General eyed Armon's pauldron. "What are you doing here, Sergeant?"

"I came here on my own volition, Sir, to investigate the presence of the gryphon."

The two men exchanged looks and nodded. The High Archon turned toward the ruins without saying a word.

"Good instincts." The General nodded, approvingly. "You are one of the three that took down the Alpha, aren't you?" He stepped to the side, gesturing toward Yara. "Are you acquainted with this creature?"

Armon looked up at her, sweating. "Yes, Sir," he said with some strain. The pressure had been becoming more intense—that frightfully familiar dread.

High General Cornelius nodded, slowly, not inquiring further. "Pity," he said in an almost solemn tone. "To lose such a capable Binder."

Yara perked, eyes wide. "RUN—" The High General cut her off with a wave of his hand, as an invisible gust of wind blasted Yara to the side, slamming her violently against the marble of wall behind her. She immediately lost consciousness.

Shocked, Armon reached for his blades, but the moment his gloved hands made contact with the handles, he froze. *That pressure—the dread—*it was suffocating him! His legs gave way and he fell to his knees. "Wh-What—" he struggled to speak, gasping for breath that his lungs refused to take in. He looked up at the two men, unable to comprehend what was happening to him.

The General drew his sword and started toward Yara.

"Let her be," the High Archon said with a raised hand. "She is no threat to us, and I would rather not invite Moira's ire."

Rocks rumbled, and Armon was now able to see him. The man that had been digging this whole time among the ruins—the source of that oppressing presence. An unnaturally tall man emerged from the ruins of marble. Muscular, bald, and dressed in gray robes. His skin—*its* skin, looked like it had been drenched in blood and then left to dry. Its eyes, deep within the eye sockets, were pitch black with red pupils, and its mouth was wolf-like wide, shaped in a nasty grin, revealing fanged teeth. It nodded respectfully toward its god, not even acknowledging Armon's struggling, hunched figure.

High Archon Feomathdar nodded back. "We will still need an Altum, but this will give us time." He waved his hand. "We are done here."

The High Archon didn't even spare Armon a glance as he passed him by. High General Cornelius came to a knee beside him, resting a hand on his slumped shoulder. "If it's of any consolation," he said. "Death isn't as bad as you may think." He remained like that for a long moment. "May you find your way into Moira's, Realm of Fae."

"Wh-why?" Armon managed to stutter.

"Sometimes," the High General paused, without looking, "I wonder the same." He rose and walked away.

The creature fell in pace behind the General, each step followed by the chime of the little bells attached on its churned staff. Armon trailed it with his eyes. *A Bloodstained—of course.* One of the Penta-pantheon's, chilling priests. The overwhelming sensation of dread that emitted from them was enough to knock a person out cold—but not kill. *So, why can't I breathe?* His eyesight started to blur as he turned toward the place the Bloodstained had been digging. A red light seemed to be pulsating from within the ruins. *I was right, wasn't I? A Blood Chasm. How brilliant of me...*

Armon looked toward Yara's small figure. She was regaining consciousness, seemingly unaffected by the Chasm—*good.* Pleased that she was still alive, he looked up at the blue, midday sky and sighed, what little air was left in his lungs dissipating. Then he smiled. *Damn it, Anthia. The one thing I regret, is never telling you how I really felt...*

"I will tell her, I promise," Yara said, struggling to her avian feet.

Armon looked at her. Smiled. Then, fell over to his side... lifeless.

Postscript

This short novella came virtually out of nowhere, and it's the first, completed piece of fiction—or otherwise—that I have ever written. By the time I had finished this (5th-July-2020), I was fully committed to writing for about six months.

I had started working on it with the intention of creating a backstory for Daren, one of the four, main characters of the Adult Fantasy novel I am currently working on, which is inspired (mostly) by Scandinavian Folklore and Greek Mythology, with a heavy emphasis on vampiric themes (more of that in the future).

It was supposed to be a ~5000 word piece (ideal chapter length) of flashbacks for Daren, describing a 'simple harpy hunt'—literally. But, as I was working on it, I came across one of my early attempts at writing as an eight-year-old. In the notes I had left on the backside of that yellowed-old textbook, I found a brief description of a Gryphon. It was so poorly written (in greek) that it actually took me a minute or two to make out what the eight-year-old me was trying to say. So, I thought, *"why not? Let's squeeze a Gryphon somewhere in there, among the harpies."* To cut the story short; one brainstorming brought the other, and the 5000 word, chapter, somehow ended up being a 12000 word, novelette, which, during editing, became a 19000 word, short novella.

Upon completing it, I realized that not only had it ended up being a three-times larger piece than I had initially intended, but that it had also had a beginning, a middle, and an end, making it a perfectly capable, standalone story with plenty of foreshadowing and subtle hints of future events and characters that I—*we.* will be revisiting.
Given that English is not my native language, I am very pleased with the result, and I cherished every moment working on it.

Thank you for taking the time to read my first ever, short story, and if you enjoyed it, know that I can leave you with a promise of more—much more—to come. We've only just scratched the surface of Illustrander's Pale Towers, Sin Binders, and Blood Chasms.

—M.G. Karabinis

About the Author

Michael G. Karabinis is a Dark Fantasy author from the Greek island of Crete, the largest island in Greece. His interests, apart from writing and reading, include video gaming, astronomy, and physics. After having received his degree in PC software programming—a profession he never pursued—and served the mandatory conscription period in the Greek armed forces, Michael began working on jobs that had nothing to do with writing. He took an interest in writing in the Summer of 2019, during a rare night-shift of low workload due to a power blackout. He had often thought of keeping a journal of his Lucid Dreams which have always been a big part of his life, as he's had them daily since he was a preschooler.

It all started with a lucid dream where three characters crossed paths inside a dark mansion and started fighting—I know, right? Following the advice of an old friend, Michael wanted to recreate that dream sequence in writing, as it had been especially vivid and exciting, setting the gears of his imagination spiraling out of control. That scene was supposed to be a single paragraph of maybe 300 words… It ended up being an oversized, full-blown chapter of 10000 words and is now acting as the genesis of his Dark Fantasy series, 'The Blood Chasms of Illustrander.' A series of novellas and novels heavily inspired by Greek Mythology and Folklore from around the world, with an emphasis on vampire themes.